WHAT'S IN FLORA'S SHOEBOX?

Words by **Sarah Jane Conklin**

Illustrations by **Venus Angelica**

Monster House Publishing
416 Northumberland St.
Fredericton NB, Canada
E3B 3K4

ISBN 978-1-77785-422-5
First Printing

Design: Danelle Vautour
Editor: Christiana Myers

Monster House Publishing acknowledges the generous support of
the Government of New Brunswick and the Department
of Tourism, Heritage and Culture.

"You cannot get through a single day without having an impact on the world around you. What you do makes a difference and you have to decide what kind of a difference you want to make."

— **Jane Goodall**

In Flora's room, beneath her bed,

Among her books and socks,

Is where her secret treasures are,

Within a small red box.

What are these keepsakes that she loves,

She's kept right from the start,

Are they from places where she's been,

Held closely to her heart?

She travelled all around the world,
Her dad right by her side,
Environmental scientists,
Their conscience was their guide.

Her knapsack packed with her supplies,
She headed out her door.
Announced in her excited voice,
"I'm ready to explore."

Observing land and animals,
They kept a busy pace.
Learned all about the planet Earth,
But hadn't left a trace.

She's watched the Arctic polar bears,
And felt the glacial air.
Ice crystals floated all around,
And formed in Flora's hair.

She's seen the deserts, hot and dry,
With golden hills of sand.
She's run her fingers through the grains,
Watched sand spill from her hand.

She's walked the beach on Fundy shores,

Found driftwood, shells, and sand.

Birds nest among the grassy dunes,

Where ocean meets the land.

She's swam in icy ocean tides,

With beach rocks soft and round.

While icebergs in the distance float,

And fishes school,

And seagulls dive,

And right whales breach unbound.

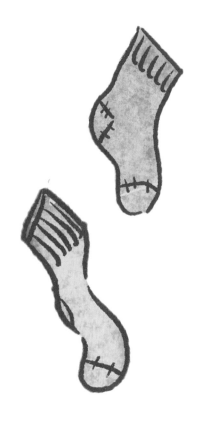

In Flora's room, beneath her bed,
Among her books and socks,
Is where her secret treasures are,
Within a small red box.
She takes them out from time to time,
And holds them in her hands.
She gently cradles every piece,
From deserts, seas, and lands.

She's walked the flooded paddy fields,
For growing crops of rice.
She's seen exotic plants and birds,
Ate grains of paradise.

She's climbed the Rockies' craggy face,

And met a mountain critter.

And with her knapsack on her back,

Camped in canyons,

Crawled in caves,

And was careful not to litter.

She's witnessed wonders of the fall,

When colours are so bold.

The maple leaves that start out green,

Then turn to red and gold.

She's played with dolphins out at sea,

Explored a coral reef.

Wild horses snorted in her face,

She laughed in disbelief.

She's hiked fjords and grassy plains,

Seen waterfalls galore.

She's trekked on trails, and walked in woods,

Ran through the rugged Cliffs of Moher,

Until her feet got sore.

She's tiptoed through some wildflower fields,
Their scent all in her wake.
So careful of the tender shoots,
She wouldn't want to break.

She's braved the jungle's wilderness,

Was drenched by heavy rain.

She drank the milk from coconuts,

And smelled the wet terrain.

She's planted trees, composted food,
And helped a calf in birth.
Reducing garbage with intent,
She healed her planet Earth.

So what's in Flora's small red box,
Come closer as I tell.
It's not so secret after all,
They're things that you know well.
Small paper notes, all gently rolled,
And wrapped up in a bow,
Of all the places in the world,
Where Flora likes to go.

All nature's treasures that she's seen,

Are left where they belong.

For taking them as souvenirs,

To Flora would be wrong.

Those trophies are not hers to take,

As proof of where she's been.

She knows what she's experienced,

As memories deep within.

For nature's gifts cannot be owned,

Or bought like any toy.

And Flora hopes they'll be preserved,

For others to enjoy.

She's older now and lives her life
With kindness, love, and truth.
Her knapsack packed, she passes on
The wisdom of her youth.

In Flora's room, beneath her bed,

Among her books and socks,

Is where her secret treasures are,

She's filling up her box.

Each tiny scroll wrapped in a bow,

Plays out a living part,

Of all the places she's explored,

Remembers,

Honours,

Loves,

Respects,

Kept stored within her heart.

THE END